Blackflies

Blackflies

Robert Munsch

illustrated by
Jay Odjick

Scholastic Canada Ltd.
Toronto New York London Auckland Sydney
Mexico City New Delhi Hong Kong Buenos Aires

Scholastic Canada Ltd.
604 King Street West, Toronto, Ontario M5V 1E1, Canada

Scholastic Inc.
557 Broadway, New York, NY 10012, USA

Scholastic Australia Pty Limited
PO Box 579, Gosford, NSW 2250, Australia

Scholastic New Zealand Limited
Private Bag 94407, Botany, Manukau 2163, New Zealand

Scholastic Children's Books
Euston House, 24 Eversholt Street, London NW1 1DB, UK

www.scholastic.ca

The artwork for this book was drawn digitally on a tablet monitor.

Library and Archives Canada Cataloguing in Publication
Munsch, Robert N., 1945-, author
Blackflies / by Robert Munsch ; illustrated by Jay Odjick.
ISBN 978-1-4431-5791-9 (softcover)
I. Odjick, Jay, illustrator II. Title.
PS8576.U575B53 2017   jC813'.54   C2016-907489-7

ISBN: 978-1-4431-5791-9

7 6 5 4 3 2   Printed in Canada   119   17 18 19 20 21

To Helen MacKay,
Fort McMurray, Alberta
—R.M.

To everyone out there writing
and drawing, no matter how
young or old, big or small, and to
everyone reading. Migwetch!
— J.O.

Helen got up very early
one morning, looked out the
window and said,
  "No snow!
  "The snow is ALL GONE!
  "I LOVE SPRINGTIME!"

She opened the front door and heard *Nnnnnnnnnnnneeeeeeeee!*

"Oh no!" said Helen. "It's the mosquitoes! It's the blackflies! They're here!

"AAHHHHHHHHHHHHHH!!" and she ran and hid under her bed.

Then she got an idea. "I think," she said, "that I will see how bad the bugs really are."

So she went to her little sister and said, "Megan, could you go outside and tell me how cold it is?"

"Well," said Megan, "I guess I can, but I get to watch MY TV SHOW when I come back."

"No problem," said Helen.

So Megan opened up the front door and ran outside in her pyjamas.

Sixteen gazillion blackflies and mosquitoes landed on her!

Megan yelled,

"AHHHHHHHHHHHHHHH!"

The sixteen gazillion blackflies and mosquitoes picked Megan up and carried her across the road to the black spruce forest where the wolves and bears live.

"Oh dear," said Helen. "The bugs are worse than I thought."

Then Helen's father came downstairs and said, "Where's Megan?"

"Well . . ." said Helen, "I think Megan is in the woods in her pyjamas."

"In her pyjamas!" yelled Helen's father. "I'm going to go get her right now." And he ran out the door in HIS pyjamas.

Helen said, "I don't think that's a good idea."

Sixteen gazillion mosquitoes and blackflies jumped on him, picked him up in the air and carried him across the road to the black spruce forest where the wolves and bears live.

"Good heavens," said Helen, "I have to do something."

So she looked for bug spray.

She found a can that said "Really Yucky Bug Glich," gave a little spritz and said, "Yuck! But not strong enough."

She found another can that said "Super Strong, Really Yucky Bug Glich," gave a little spritz and said, "Yuck! But still not strong enough."

She found another can that said
"Super Strong, Extra Yucky, Even
Knocks Out Wolves Bug Glich," gave
a little spritz and said,
"YUCK! GLACK! GLUBAHHH!
That's strong enough."

Then Helen ran across the street and into the woods, spraying the bug spray in front of her.

She came to a big pile of blackflies and mosquitoes. From underneath, something was yelling, *"Ooooowwww! Aaaaah! Ooooowwww Aaaaah!"*

Helen sprayed the pile for a while and finally the blackflies and mosquitoes flew away. Underneath was a wolf, and Helen was spraying the bug spray right into the wolf's face.

The wolf yelled, **"YUCK! GLACK! GLUBAHHH!"** and fell over.

"Sorry," said Helen.

Helen walked some more and she came to a bigger pile of blackflies and mosquitoes. From underneath, something was yelling, *"Oooowwww! Aaaaah! Oooowwww Aaaaah!"*

Helen sprayed that pile for a while and finally the blackflies and mosquitoes flew away. Underneath was a bear, and Helen was spraying the bug spray right in the bear's face.

The bear yelled,

"YUCK! GLACK! GLUBAHHH!"
and fell over.

"Sorry," said Helen.

Helen walked some more and she came to another pile of blackflies and mosquitoes. From underneath, something was yelling, *"Oooowwww! Aaaaah! Oooowwww Aaaaah!"*

Helen sprayed that pile for a while and finally the blackflies and mosquitoes flew away. Underneath was Megan, and Helen was spraying the bug spray right in her face.

Megan yelled,

"YUCK! GLACK! GLUBAHHH!"
and ran around bumping into trees.

"Sorry," said Helen.

Helen and Megan went farther into the woods until they found another big pile of mosquitoes and blackflies. It was jumping up and down, yelling, *"Oooowwww! Aaaaah! Oooowwww Aaaaah!"*

"I hope," said Helen, "that this is my dad. I do not want to meet another bear."

Helen sprayed that pile for a while and finally the blackflies and mosquitoes flew away. There was Helen's dad, and Helen was spraying the bug spray right in his face. He yelled,

"YUCK! GLACK! GLUBAHHH!"

"Sorry," said Helen.

And they all stood still and heard a sound like this:

Nnnnnnnnnnnneeeeeeeeeeeeeeeee!

That was sixty-four gazillion mosquitoes and blackflies getting ready to come back, because they had decided that they LIKED the bug spray.

"RUN!" yelled Helen's dad, and they all ran really fast through the woods, across the road, through the front yard, and into the house.

Then after breakfast they all came out wearing bug jackets and bug hats and went for a walk in the woods, because it was, after all, springtime.

But, unfortunately, there are no hats or jackets to keep away BEARS!